THREATENING SKIES!
HISTORY'S MOST DANGEROUS WEATHER

by Suzanne Garbe

Consultant:
Dr. Vladimir Jankovic, President
International Commission on History of Meteorology
Boston, Massachusetts

CAPSTONE PRESS
a capstone imprint

Edge Books are published by Capstone Press,
1710 Roe Crest Drive, North Mankato, Minnesota 56003
www.capstonepub.com

Copyright © 2014 by Capstone Press, a Capstone imprint. All rights reserved.
No part of this publication may be reproduced in whole or in part, or stored
in a retrieval system, or transmitted in any form or by any means, electronic,
mechanical, photocopying, recording, or otherwise, without written
permission of the publisher.

Library of Congress Cataloging-in-Publication Data
Garbe, Suzanne, author.
 Threatening skies!: history's most dangerous weather / by Suzanne Garbe.
  pages cm. — (Edge. Dangerous history)
 Summary: "Describes several of the most dangerous weather events in
recorded history"— Provided by publisher.
 Includes bibliographical references and index.
 ISBN 978-1-4765-0128-4 (library binding)
 ISBN 978-1-4765-3384-1 (ebook pdf)
 1. Weather—Juvenile literature. 2. Storms—Juvenile literature. 3. Natural
disasters—History—Juvenile literature. I. Title.
QC981.3.G376 2014
551.5—dc23   2013009485

Editorial Credits
Mandy Robbins, editor; Sarah Bennett, designer; Marcie Spence,
media researcher; Charmaine Whitman, production specialist

Photo Credits
AP Images: Cecil County Dept. of Emergency Management, 9, Harry
Koundakjian, 27, NOAA George E. Marsh Album, 23; Bridgeman Art Library:
Bibliotheque Nationale, Paris, France, 13; Capstone, 11; Getty Images:
David L. Nelson/AFP, 21, Edward Miller/Keystone/Hulton Archive, 7, Marko
Georgiev, 25, Stock Montage, 15, Wallace G. Levinson/Time Life Pictures, 16;
Shutterstock: Adam Gryko, 17, Amgun, design element, andreiuc88, cover
(bottom left), B747, 19 (top), Daniel Loretto, cover (top right), filmfoto,
cover (bottom left), lolloj, design element, Nejron Photo, cover (bottom
right), Norman B, 19 (bottom), Perspectives – Jeff Smith, 5, pio3, cover
(middle right), romarti, 1, Sandy MacKenzie, 28–29, Valentin Agapov, design
element, Zastolskiy Victor, cover (top left)

Printed in the United States of America in Stevens Point, Wisconsin.
032013   007227WZF13

TABLE OF CONTENTS

When Weather Turns Deadly 4

Killer Fog 6

Deadliest Lightning Strike................8

Yangtze River Flood of 1931.............10

The Hailstorm that Turned a War 12

The Snowstorm that
Stopped New York City 14

The Great Hurricane of 1780 18

The World's Deadliest Tornado...........20

The Dust Bowl 22

Hurricane Katrina 24

The Deadliest Cyclone 26

TIMELINE 28

GLOSSARY.............................30

READ MORE 31

INTERNET SITES........................31

INDEX................................32

WEATHER TURNS

Snow has been falling for days, and cars are sliding into ditches. Lightning is spotted in the sky, and the big game is canceled. Luckily, minor events like these make up many people's worst experiences with weather. But other people haven't been so lucky. Throughout history, humans have faced deadly weather.

Weather is defined as the conditions in the **atmosphere** at any given time. Conditions include sunshine, clouds, rain, and wind. Most of the time the weather is fairly calm. But sometimes it becomes dangerous. Tornadoes, hurricanes, floods, sandstorms, rainstorms, extreme heat, and snowstorms can all have a deadly impact on human life.

Many of history's most destructive weather events have happened in the last 200 years. This is partly because people didn't keep weather records until recently. Another reason is that the Earth's population is growing and so are the cities people live in. As the population increases, it's more likely weather will impact a greater number of lives and destroy more property.

FACT

At any given moment, approximately 2,000 thunderstorms are raging across our planet.

A tornado can destroy an entire neighborhood in minutes.

atmosphere—the blanket of gases that surrounds a planet

LONDON, ENGLAND • DECEMBER 5-9, 1952

People in big cities often complain about air quality. But today's air **pollution** is minor compared to what residents of London, England, faced in December 1952.

In 1952 coal was used for heating London's homes and powering its factories. Burning coal created high levels of pollution in the air. On December 5, it was made worse by a thick cloud of fog in the city. High **air pressure** and low wind caused the smoke and fog to stay put. It hung around the city and seeped into buildings. Concert halls and sports stadiums closed. Buses stopped running. Airplanes had to land in other cities. The chemical-filled fog made thousands of people sick.

A strong wind blew the fog away four days later. By that time, more than 4,000 people had died. Lingering health problems created by the fog caused another 8,000 people to die after it lifted. Most of the people who died were elderly or already had breathing problems.

pollution—materials that hurt Earth's water, air, and land

air pressure—the weight of air pushing against something

"It's like you were blind."
— Stan Cribb, London resident

CECIL COUNTY, MARYLAND · DECEMBER 8, 1963

A sleepy Maryland town was jolted awake one rainy night in 1963. On December 8, a storm rumbled in the sky. Pan American Airways Flight 214 circled overhead. It was waiting to land at the airport in nearby Philadelphia, Pennsylvania, when lightning struck the plane. The plane crashed into a cornfield. The last communication from the pilot was, "Mayday, mayday, mayday, clipper 214 out of control. Here we go … " Emergency workers rushed to the site, but it was too late to save the 81 people onboard.

Today lightning strikes commercial airliners about once each year. But the strikes are no longer a serious threat. Pan Am Flight 214 and other airplane crashes inspired scientists to better protect airplanes from lightning strikes. Today's planes are made of materials that let lightning pass through a plane without harming anything. The crash of Pan Am Flight 214 stands in the record books as the deadliest known lightning strike in history.

"A [piece of] **fuselage** with about eight or 10 window frames was about the only large recognizable piece I could see when I pulled up. It was just a **debris** field. It didn't resemble an airplane."

—Don Hash, emergency responder

FACT

The country of Rwanda in Africa is known as the "lightning capital of the world." On average, each square mile of Rwanda is struck by lightning 50 times per year.

fuselage—the main body of an airplane

debris—the scattered pieces of something that has been broken or destroyed

CHINA • JULY-AUGUST 1931

Floods typically happen in one of two ways. Inland floods are usually a result of too much rain. Floods in coastal areas often happen when storms sweep in seawater. Floods can be made worse by man-made factors such as **levee** failures.

The Yangtze River flood in 1931 had natural causes. From April to August, storms dropped huge amounts of rain onto a highly populated area of China. The Yangtze River overflowed its banks, flooding towns and farmland. People died during and after the flood. Floodwater contaminated drinking water and spread disease. It also ruined farmland, which meant people couldn't grow enough food to eat. As a result, the Yangtze River flood caused 3.7 million deaths from drowning, disease, and starvation.

levee—an embankment built to prevent a body of water from overflowing

In 1931 the Yangtze River surged over its banks, destroying everything in its path.

FACT

Floods are the most common and deadliest of all natural disasters. They cause 40 percent of all deaths from natural disasters.

THE HAILSTORM THAT TURNED A WAR

FRANCE • APRIL 1360

Ice storms are made up of sleet and **hail**. One of the most significant hailstorms in history occurred in 1360 near Chartres, France. This was early in the Hundred Years War, which Britain and France fought for control of France. The British army had captured a series of French towns when a storm hit. According to records, the storm dropped hailstones as large as goose eggs on the British army. Within minutes 10,000 men and 6,000 horses were battered to death by the hail. The British forces retreated and made a temporary peace agreement with France shortly after.

FACT
Hailstones form inside clouds when super-cold water attaches to small ice crystals. The hailstones are carried by wind inside the clouds. Golf ball-sized hailstones grow for about 10 minutes before becoming heavy enough to fall to earth.

hail—balls of ice that may fall during thunderstorms

a battle scene from the Hundred Years War

STOPPED NEW YORK CITY

NORTHEASTERN UNITED STATES • MARCH 11-14, 1888

Before modern forecasting, weather events could be extra dangerous because people weren't warned about them. That's what happened in New York City in March 1888. A light rain began falling on March 11. By the following day, the rain had turned to snow. No one knew how bad it would get or how long it would continue.

The snow became a four-day **blizzard**, now known as the "Great Blizzard of 1888." Snowdrifts reached almost 20 feet (6 meters) high. Most cities up and down the East Coast lost power and means of transportation. The wind tore off roofs. Families were exposed to the cold and snow. In New York City, some families lit fires that ended up burning down their houses. Fire departments couldn't be reached to help.

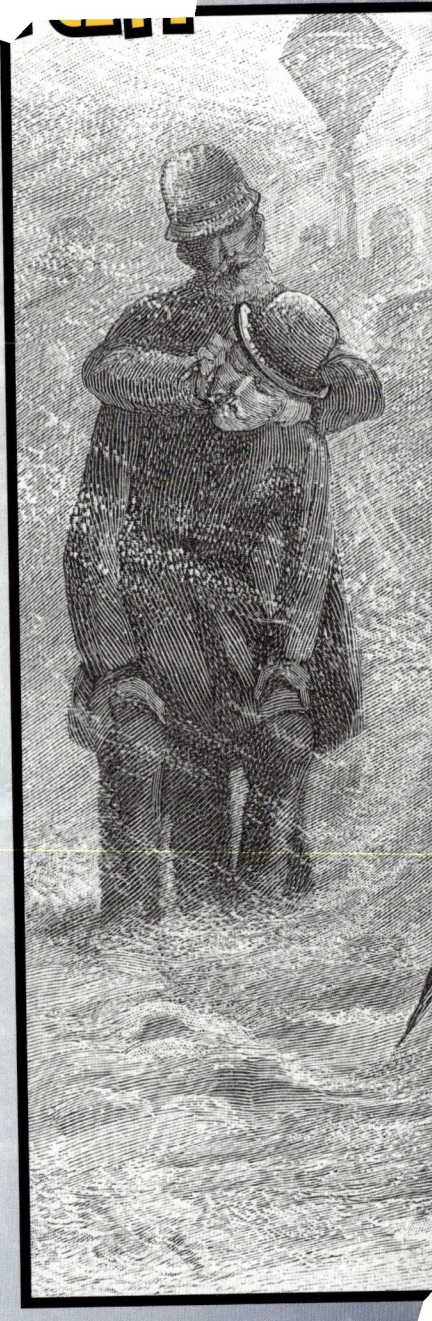

blizzard—a heavy snowstorm with strong wind; a blizzard can last several days

The storm stretched across the northeastern United States. The highest recorded snowfall during the storm was 58 inches (147 centimeters) in Sarasota Springs, New York. In other towns, winds reached 80 miles (129 kilometers) per hour. Three-story houses were completely covered by snowdrifts.

On March 14, the snow stopped and it soon melted. But it took months for power to be restored and debris to be cleared. In all, 400 people died.

On March 14, 1888, New York City residents flocked to the streets to survey the storm damage.

The same year the Great Blizzard roared across the Northeast, the Midwest experienced its own tragic storm. On January 11, weather across the central United States had been unusually warm. The next day, temperatures dropped by as much as 100 degrees Fahrenheit (38 degrees Celsius). A severe blizzard hit with no warning. Temperatures in North Dakota plunged to -40°F (-40°C).

The blinding storm came during the day, trapping many children in one-room schoolhouses. In one South Dakota town, adults tied a rope from a schoolhouse to the closest warm shelter. Students followed the rope to safety. But other children were not so lucky. In Plainfield, Nebraska, three schoolchildren died trying to find a home less than 90 yards (82 meters) from their school. These tragic deaths gave the storm its name: the Schoolchildren's Blizzard. It's believed that 235 people died in the storm.

The Great Hurricane of 1780

CARIBBEAN ISLANDS • OCTOBER 10-12, 1780

The deadliest Atlantic Hurricane on record is the Great Hurricane of 1780. It passed through the Caribbean islands of Martinique, St. Lucia, St. Vincent, St. Eustatius, Barbados, and Puerto Rico.

Each island reported many deaths, with some reports into the thousands. The whole island of Martinique was devastated. The storm arrived on Barbados at night. Entire families were killed as they slept in their homes. Winds reached up to 200 miles (322 km) per hour. The storm destroyed every tree and building on Barbados.

The storm also tore across the ocean and ripped apart boats. Thousands of French soldiers drowned in ships anchored in the Caribbean Sea. In all, the death toll ranged from 20,000 to 22,000.

When hurricanes hit land, they bring huge, destructive waves.

TORNADO

BANGLADESH • APRIL 26, 1989

The world's deadliest tornado was relatively small and lasted just minutes. But it hit an area with a high population that was not prepared for it.

In late April 1989, Bangladesh was suffering from a two-month **drought**. On April 26, the nation's president asked people to pray for rain. Hours later it began to fall. But with the rain came something much worse: the deadliest tornado in recorded history.

The tornado tore through central Bangladesh. In just 10 minutes, it destroyed every structure within 2.3 square miles (6 square km). The tornado's path was 10 miles (16 km) long and 1 mile (1.6 km) wide. More than 20 villages were destroyed and 12,000 people were injured. The tornado killed about 1,300 people.

drought—a long period of weather with little or no rainfall

"*I saw black clouds gathering in the sky. In moments we found we were flying along with the house.*"
— Sayeda Begum, 1989 Bangladesh tornado survivor

People survey the damage in the aftermath of the April 1989 tornado that hit Bangladesh.

UNITED STATES • 1934-1941

Droughts, heat waves, and a series of dust storms hit the central United States during the 1930s. Strong winds blew away **topsoil** and lifted it into clouds stretching 1,000 feet (305 m) into the sky. The clouds blocked out the sun. Wind gusts reached 60 miles (97 km) per hour. The wind blew so much dirt into the nostrils of cattle that they **suffocated**.

Along with the strong winds, rain was rare, and temperatures were high. The seeds farmers planted never sprouted. About 25,000 square miles (64,750 square km) of land turned into a wasteland of dust where crops couldn't grow. Temperatures reached 110°F (43°C) and stayed there for days.

These horrible weather events happened during a period of hard times in the United States called the Great Depression. The Dust Bowl made the Great Depression even worse for many people. More than 300,000 Americans were forced to leave their homes to look for work.

topsoil—the top layer of soil that is best for planting

suffocate—to die from lack of oxygen

"You got inside the house quick, watched the cloud coming, and felt it envelop you. I've known storms to last 12 hours. Dirt clicked like sleet against the window glass."

— Lawrence Svobida, Dust Bowl survivor

SOUTHEASTERN UNITED STATES • AUGUST 25-31, 2005

Hurricane Katrina started as a tropical storm on August 23, 2005. The storm threatened to hit the entire Gulf Coast area.

New Orleans, Louisiana, was especially at risk. The city's average elevation is 6 feet (1.8 m) below sea level. On August 28, New Orleans mayor Ray Nagin ordered all residents to **evacuate** the city. But it was already too late. Hurricane Katrina made landfall the next day, before many people had a chance to escape.

Katrina knocked out power and destroyed homes all over the Gulf Coast. Wind speeds reached 120 miles (193 km) per hour. The area was pelted with 15 inches (38 cm) of rain. The 20-foot (6-m) **storm surge** made the situation even worse. The levees failed. Much of New Orleans and many other cities were flooded.

Katrina took 1,836 lives and left about 1 million people homeless. The states of Alabama, Florida, Louisiana, and Mississippi were declared disaster areas. The cleanup for the storm cost $123 billion dollars.

> **evacuate**—to leave an area during a time of danger
>
> **storm surge**—a huge wave of water pushed ashore by an approaching hurricane

New Orleans residents wait on their roofs to be rescued after their homes were flooded during Hurricane Katrina.

"We grabbed a lady and pulled her out the window and then we swam with the current. It was terrifying. You should have seen the cars floating around us. We had to push them away when we were trying to swim."

— Joy Schovest, Hurricane Katrina survivor

EAST PAKISTAN (PRESENT-DAY BANGLADESH) · NOVEMBER 12-13, 1970

In October 1970, people in East Pakistan were warned of a tropical **cyclone** about to hit. Pakistan's national radio station, Radio Pakistan, broadcast warnings. Many people evacuated their homes. In the end, though, the storm was mild. People returned home, frustrated that they'd left for nothing.

When warnings about another cyclone reached Radio Pakistan several weeks later, the station ignored them. This left the citizens unprepared for the terrible storm that hit while they slept on November 12. The strong winds caused a storm surge at least 20 feet (6 m) tall. Thousands of people were swept out to sea while they slept. Houses were destroyed, and power lines were torn down.

After the storm, diseases spread across the area. In total, between 300,000 and 500,000 people died. Many people consider this cyclone the worst natural disaster of the 1900s.

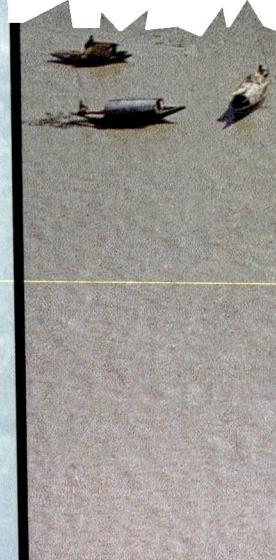

The November 1970 cyclone tore apart buildings and devastated communities in East Pakistan.

cyclone—a storm with strong winds that blow around a center

Millions of lives have been lost to weather events throughout history. But lives have also been saved by modern weather forecasting, warning systems, and well-built structures. Advanced technology helps keep us safe. We might be able to outsmart the weather sometimes, but we can never stop its awe-inspiring power.

TIMELINE

APRIL 1360
A huge hailstorm halts the Hundred Years War in France.

JANUARY 12, 1888
The Schoolchildren's Blizzard is a deadly surprise to people in the midwestern United States.

OCTOBER 10-12, 1780
The Great Hurricane devastates islands in the Atlantic Ocean.

MARCH 11-14, 1888
A deadly blizzard hits the northeastern United States, shutting down New York City.

1907
A horrible drought kills 24 million people in China.

MARCH 18, 1925
The deadliest U.S. tornado, also called the Tri-State Tornado, hits the midwestern United States.

OCTOBER 29-30, 2012
Hurricane Sandy shuts down the mid-Atlantic and northeastern United States.

AUGUST 25-30, 2005
Hurricane Katrina devastates the Gulf Coast of the United States.

APRIL 26, 1989
The deadliest tornado in recorded history touches down in Bangladesh.

NOVEMBER 12-13, 1970
The deadliest tropical cyclone kills 300,000 to 500,000 people in East Pakistan, which is now Bangladesh.

DECEMBER 8, 1963
The deadliest lightning strike in history causes Pan Am Flight 214 to crash in Maryland.

DECEMBER 5-9, 1952
A deadly fog takes over London, England.

1934-1941
The Dust Bowl takes out the farming industry in the midwestern United States.

JULY-AUGUST 1931
The deadliest flood in recorded history devastates China.

29

GLOSSARY

air pressure (AYR PRESH-uhr)—the weight of air pushing against something

atmosphere (AT-muhss-fihr)—the blanket of gases that surrounds a planet

blizzard (BLIZ-urd)—a heavy snowstorm with strong wind; a blizzard can last several days

cyclone (SY-clohn)—a storm with strong winds that blow around a center

debris (duh-BREE)—the scattered pieces of something that has been broken or destroyed

drought (DROUT)—a long period of weather with little or no rainfall

evacuate (i-VAK-yoo-ate)—to leave an area during a time of danger

fuselage (FYOO-suh-lahzh)—the main body of an airplane

hail (HAYL)—balls of ice that may fall during thunderstorms

levee (LEV-ee)—an embankment built to prevent a body of water from overflowing

pollution (puh-LOO-shuhn)—materials that hurt Earth's water, air, and land

storm surge (STORM SURJ)—a huge wave of water pushed ashore by an approaching hurricane

suffocate (SUHF-uh-kate)—to die from lack of oxygen

topsoil (TOP-soil)—the top layer of soil that is best for planting

READ MORE

Dougherty, Terri. *The Worst Hurricanes of All Time.* Epic Disasters. Mankato, Minn.: Capstone Press, 2012.

Leet, Karen M. *This Book Might Blow You Away: A Collection of Amazing Weather Trivia.* Super Trivia Collection. North Mankato, Minn.: Capstone Press, 2013.

Mogil, H. Michae, and Barbara G. Levine. *Extreme Weather.* Insiders. New York: Simon & Schuster, 2011.

Reilly, Kathleen M. *Explore Weather and Climate!* White River Junction, Vt.: Nomad, 2012.

INTERNET SITES

FactHound offers a safe, fun way to find Internet sites related to this book. All of the sites on FactHound have been researched by our staff.

Here's all you do:

Visit *www.facthound.com*

Type in this code: 9781476501284

Check out projects, games and lots more at
www.capstonekids.com

INDEX

airplanes, 6, 8–9, 29

Bangladesh, 20, 26, 29
blizzards, 14–17, 28

cyclones, 26, 29

droughts, 20, 22, 28
Dust Bowl, 22–23, 29

floods, 4, 10, 11, 24, 29
fog, 6, 29
forecasting, 14, 28

hail, 12, 28
Hundred Years War, 12, 28
Hurricane Katrina, 24–25, 29
hurricanes, 4, 18, 24, 25, 28, 29

lightning, 4, 8, 9, 29

New Orleans, 24
New York City, 14, 16, 28

Pan Am Flight 214, 8–9, 29
pollution, 6

rain, 4, 8, 10, 14, 20, 22, 24

snow, 4, 14, 16
storm surge, 24, 26

thunderstorms, 5, 8
tornadoes, 4, 20, 28, 29

wind, 4, 6, 12, 14, 16, 18, 22, 24, 26

Yangtze River, 10